Alexander Christmas 1988
with love from
George and Harriette.

'"TIGERS ESCAPE!" said the newspapers on Monday morning. "TIGER HUNT BEGINS!"

Alix hardly dared read what the papers had to say. She could scarcely believe that she had played a part in it, but there it was in big letters on the front page of the paper. Underneath the headline was a picture of Mah-Var and Mah-Baja and a warning to stay well clear of them.

The zoo had no explanation.'

Only Alix knows how the tigers managed to escape – and she is glad that they are free, for they are old and gentle and can't hurt anyone. But then a cruel hunter arrives and Alix knows that she must act fast if she is to save the two tigers . . .

FOR JAN AND NICOLA
VAN ZLY SMIT

Also by Alexander McCall Smith and published by Young Corgi Books:
MIKE'S MAGIC SEEDS

BY MYSELF books are specially selected to be suitable for beginner readers. Other BY MYSELF books available from Young Corgi Books include:

TRUANT FROM SPACE by Brian Ball
THE BIG OLD HORSE by Evelyn Davies
T.R. BEAR: T.R. AFLOAT by Terrance Dicks
URSULA SAILING by Sheila Lavelle
THE AMAZING PET by Marjorie Newman
DRAGON EARTH by Ann Ruffell

ALEXANDER McCALL SMITH

Illustrated by Jon Miller

YOUNG CORGI BOOKS

ALIX AND THE TIGERS
A YOUNG CORGI BOOK 0 552 524778

Originally published in Great Britain by Young Corgi Books

PRINTING HISTORY
Young Corgi edition published 1988

This book is set in 14/18 pt Century by Colset Private Limited, Singapore.

Young Corgi Books are published by Transworld Publishers Ltd., 61-63 Uxbridge Road, Ealing, London W5 5SA, in Australia by Transworld Publishers (Australia) Pty. Ltd., 15-23 Helles Avenue, Moorebank, NSW 2170, and in New Zealand by Transworld Publishers (N.Z.) Ltd., Cnr. Moselle and Waipareira Avenues, Henderson, Auckland.

Made and printed in Great Britain by
The Guernsey Press Co. Ltd., Guernsey, Channel Islands.

Chapter One

The only important thing in Alix's town was a zoo. Other towns had parks and lakes, or even fun-fairs which people liked to visit, but Alix's town had none of these. There was just the zoo.

It wouldn't have been so bad if it

had been a good zoo, but it wasn't. The cages were old and rather small. The animals looked as if they didn't have quite enough to eat. And everywhere you went in this zoo there was a bit of a smell.

In spite of all these drawbacks, Alix still enjoyed visiting the zoo. She loved to walk along the narrow paths between the cages and the paddocks. She loved to watch the monkeys in the monkey house as they swung from branch to branch and made faces at the people. She loved to watch the penguins being fed. There was always a lot going on, although it wasn't a very good zoo.

As well as having smaller animals, this zoo had a number of larger

beasts. There were two Indian elephants. They were very large and very old. They didn't walk very much any more, but stood under a tree and looked as if they were crying. Then there were a couple of giraffes. They used to be extremely tall but now seemed to have become bent with age. Most of the time they seemed to be asleep.

The most unhappy-looking of the larger animals, however, were the two tigers. They were called Mah-Var and Mah-Baja, and they paced their cage all day as if they were looking for a way out. They wore their stripes with pride, but like all the other animals they were thin and rickety. Underneath their skins, where muscles should have rippled in waves, you could see the bones sticking out; at the very ends of their handsome feet, where the claws should have looked like wicked needles, there were little white stubs. And their teeth, which should have gleamed white even in the dark, were yellowed and blunt.

They were very unhappy. As they paced their cage (which was too small for such large animals), or as they lay panting on hot days, they thought of the jungle from which they had been taken as cubs. It was a long time ago, but they still wished for their freedom.

Alix would stand in front of the cage and watch the two tigers inside. A thick pane of glass separated her from the two wild animals, but still she felt afraid. If the glass were not there it would be so easy for the tigers to take one leap and land at her feet. And if that happened . . . Well, she could barely bring herself to imagine it. What would it be like to be eaten by a tiger? Would it hurt a great deal, or would it be over quickly, like having a tooth pulled out by the dentist? Would it take the tigers two bites to eat her, or three? What would they do with her toes? These were the questions she asked herself while the tigers watched her from the corners of their big, dark eyes.

Of course these two tigers were not in the slightest bit dangerous. Alix had watched one of the keepers clean-

ing out their cage one day and had seen that he took hardly any notice of the tigers prowling around behind him. When Mah-Var came up beside him and snarled, showing his old yellow teeth, the keeper had merely tapped him on the nose with his broom.

To Alix's surprise, the tiger had run off whimpering, tail between his legs.

Later she had asked the keeper whether it had been safe for him to go into the cage.

'Good heavens!' the keeper had replied with a laugh. 'Shall I let you in on a secret? Those old creatures may look like tigers, but they're really no more dangerous than kittens. And that,' he went on, smiling, 'is not very dangerous, is it?'

Chapter Two

It was a Saturday afternoon. Alix had gone to the zoo with two of her friends. They liked to spend all their time in the monkey house, and so she had left them there to go and look at the other animals. The elephants were doing nothing, so she did not stay long with them. The giraffes were standing still, their heads drooping down, so she quickly said goodbye to them too. That left the tigers.

Mah-Var was gnawing at a bone, his teeth making a horrible grating sound as he bit. Mah-Baja was asleep, spread over the tree-trunk that lay in the middle of their cage. Alix stood in front of the glass barrier and stared at the tigers. Then, gently, she tapped on the glass to see if she could make Mah-Baja wake up.

Mah-Baja opened one eye and then closed it. She tried to snarl, but she was so tired that it sounded more like a hiccup. That would have to do. It was difficult to behave like a real tiger when you lived in a cage like that.

Alix watched Mah-Baja lying on her tree-trunk. She felt sorry for her. It was sad to see her in her little cage. How dull life must be for her. If only she could get out. If only she could climb a real tree, not an old tree-trunk which had no leaves and which was beginning to rot.

Alix looked at her watch. It was getting late and the zoo was due to close in a few minutes. She would have to find her friends in the monkey house and tell them it was time to go home. She began to walk away from the tiger cage, past the large iron door through which the keepers threw the tigers their meat. She stopped. She had noticed something very unusual indeed. The door of the tigers' cage,

which was usually kept firmly locked, was open. It was only ever so slightly ajar, but a push, even a little one, would open it.

Alix thought for a moment. The keepers, who were usually so careful, had this time been careless. If a tiger were to bump against the door . . . She looked around. No keeper was in sight. Should she go to the office to call one? Or should she leave it? Would it matter all that much if the tigers escaped? She knew that they would never harm anyone and it would be good for them to have some freedom again. Yes, why not? Why shouldn't the tigers be free again, even if only for a day or so?

Without saying anything about the

open door, Alix left the cage behind her and went to join her friends.

'Goodbye,' she whispered to the tigers under her breath. 'Enjoy yourselves!'

Chapter Three

'TIGERS ESCAPE!' said the newspaper on Monday morning. 'TIGER HUNT BEGINS!'

Alix hardly dared read what the paper had to say. She could scarcely believe that she had played a part in it, but there it was in big letters on the front page of the paper. Underneath the headline was a picture of Mah-Var and Mah-Baja and a warning to stay well clear of them.

The zoo had no explanation.

'We don't know how they got out,' the tiger-keeper said. 'Their cage is very strong and the walls are high. They couldn't have jumped.'

Alix smiled. What a fuss was being made over the escape of two tigers who couldn't harm anybody, even if they wanted to. Of course the keepers would have to say that the tigers were dangerous. Who would want to visit a zoo where even the tigers were too old and run-down to be dangerous?

She wondered where they were now? She hoped that they were in one of the nearby woods, prowling through the trees, pretending they were back in India. She hoped that they had enjoyed running away from the zoo, feeling the fresh grass beneath their feet for the first time in years. She hoped that they were happy, wherever they were.

Although Alix didn't know it, Mah-Var and Mah-Baja were not far away. Right at the edge of the town there was a large wood, thick and dark, an ideal place for tigers. They had made their way into this wood on the very night of their escape and had found a comfortable, dry place to sleep. They were happier than they had ever been in their lives. Above them, through the criss-cross of the branches, they could see the night sky and the stars. Beneath them was a bed of leaves, real leaves from real trees. And all about them was the open air, with no fences, no glass barriers, no people standing and staring.

The next morning, just as the sun came up, they made their way to a farmyard. Nobody was about and it was a simple job, even for two rickety old tigers, to pounce on a couple of ducks and carry them off into a field. After that meal, they caught a few chickens and enjoyed them too. Then, their bellies comfortably full, they walked slowly down the lane, their creaky old legs clicking with each step.

It was as they strolled round a

corner that they met their first person. When Mah-Var saw the man on his bicycle, he uttered as loud a roar as he could. It was not much of a roar by the standards of other tigers, but it was frightening enough for the cyclist. Fumbling and wobbling, he turned his bicycle round and pedalled furiously away.

Mah-Baja decided to give chase. Her stride was slow, but she just managed to catch up with the bicycle and bite the back wheel. As she did so, the spokes of the turning wheel knocked out two of her teeth, while a third stuck in the bicycle tyre. The cyclist yelped in fright but continued pedalling. Mah-Baja gave a little howl as she felt the teeth fall out. Her eyes

watering from the pain, she sat down to get back her breath and watch the disappearing bicycle. Her gums felt very sore indeed but it had been good to chase something again after all those years.

Chapter Four

When the news got round that one of the tigers had bitten a bicycle, everybody started to make a fuss. Posters appeared in the town, offering a reward for the recapture of the tigers. People kept their doors and windows closed. Nobody felt safe. If you walked about in the streets, you kept throwing a glance over your shoulder, just in case.

Alix, of course, wasn't in the least bit frightened. She knew that the tigers were harmless and that if people just left them alone they would cause no trouble. She began to worry, though, when she heard that the zoo had decided that somebody had actually opened the tigers' cage door.

'The culprit must be found,' the newspaper said. 'Whoever let those tigers out deserves to be punished very severely indeed!'

Alix began to wonder whether she had made a mistake. All she had done was to keep quiet about the open door, and that she had done to help the tigers. People had no right to keep animals in those conditions – that zoo didn't deserve to have tigers. At the same time, there was no doubt that everybody was very angry. If they found out that she had deliberately done nothing then she could imagine the trouble she'd be in. Was saying nothing about an open door as bad as actually opening the door? Perhaps it was.

It was difficult to keep the secret to herself, and at last she decided to tell a friend.

'I wonder how the tigers really got out,' her friend John remarked. 'I bet they jumped.'

'They didn't,' Alix replied. 'They got out through the door of their cage.'

'Nonsense,' John retorted. 'Their door is always locked. I've seen the keeper lock it after feeding time.'

Alix shook her head. 'It wasn't locked that day.'

'Oh yes?' John sneered. 'And how would you know that?'

'I just know,' Alix replied simply.

John laughed. 'You don't know what you're talking about.'

'I do,' said Alix quickly. 'I saw it myself.'

John stared at his friend. 'And you did nothing?' he asked.

Alix gulped. She had given the secret away and she immediately regretted it. Still, it was too late now and she decided to go on.

'I felt so sorry for them,' she

explained. 'It seemed wrong to coop them up in that awful cage. How would you like to have so little space, if you were a tiger?' She paused. 'And so I didn't say anything.'

John whistled. 'You're in deep trouble,' he said, his voice full of warning. 'You should have told the keepers.'

Alix laughed. 'I don't see why,' she said airily. 'The tigers have got away. They won't harm anyone. And nobody will find out that I knew.'

John shook his head in disbelief. 'It was really wrong of you to do that. You were really . . . really . . .' He searched for the right word. 'Really . . . stupid.'

'That's what you think,' Alix replied. 'I'm sure the tigers don't

think that.'

John glared at her. 'And what if they eat somebody? What then?'

'They won't,' said Alix. 'They couldn't.'

John kept staring at Alix. 'You'll have to catch them,' he said at last. 'You're to blame for their being out in the first place, so you'd better catch them.'

'No,' said Alix. 'I won't.'

John shook his finger at her. 'You've got one week to catch them again,' he said. 'And if you don't I'm going to tell everybody it was you!'

Chapter Five

The zoo did its best to catch the tigers. The keepers set out in trucks laden with nets, searching in all the parks and all the gardens, prodding about in dark corners, ready with the little tranquillizing darts that would put the tigers to sleep the moment they were struck by one.

There were many sightings phoned through to the zoo. One man saw a tiger crouching behind a tree in the town park; another saw what he called a 'stripy sort of creature' drinking from the fishpond at the bottom of his garden. And one old lady, who was a bit nervous about this sort of thing, was certain that one, if not both of the tigers, was under her bed.

'I'm sure they're there,' she said to the keeper who came in response to her call. 'I heard them. I'm sure I did.'

Two days after the tigers had escaped, a large meeting was held in the town hall. It was addressed by the mayor, a stout man with a large, wavy moustache. Just about everybody

was there, all waiting for the mayor to tell them what he planned to do about the tigers.

'We shall have to do something soon,' the mayor began. 'The zoo doesn't seem to be getting anywhere in finding these tigers. We can't have wild animals running about the place. It will do the town no good at all!'

There was much nodding of heads from the audience. In the back row, somebody cheered.

'So,' said the mayor. 'So, we shall have to take action. I mean to say, we shall not just stand about doing nothing.'

'No!' shouted a man at the back. 'We can't do nothing.'

'Indeed,' said the mayor quickly.

'Nothing can be done. I mean, nothing can't be done. And so . . . and so . . . I suggest we think of something to do.'

And with that he sat down. At first there was loud applause, but slowly this died away and was followed by deep silence. The mayor looked down at his shoes, then up at the ceiling. The man at the back coughed and several people blew their noses noisily.

Then a woman in the middle called out.

'We need to get together in a group and go out and look for them,' she said.

'Good idea!' somebody shouted out.

'We could just round them up,' another said. 'Then we'd take them back to the zoo.'

There were murmurs of agreement, followed by silence.

'How?' asked a quiet voice. 'How do we round them up?'

Nobody knew the answer and the whole hall broke out into furious argument. Everybody wanted to blame somebody else. Some said it was the mayor's fault; some said it was all the fault of the keepers at the zoo. Others said that the tigers shouldn't have been there in the first place. Nobody, however, had anything useful to say. It was at this point that the rear door of the hall was flung open and there, in the doorway, stood a tall man with a thin face and with eyes which looked just like a rat's.

'Good evening,' the stranger said to the quietened hall. 'I understand you have a little problem.'

Nobody answered him. There was something about him which overawed them all and which made them unwilling to speak out.

The stranger smiled, a thin, tight-lipped smile. 'Well,' he said. 'Perhaps I should introduce myself. But first, let me ask you a question. What do you think I do for my living? Can anyone answer that?'

Nobody spoke. All eyes were fixed on the cruel mouth and the flashing black eyes of the strange newcomer.

'Well,' he said. 'I shall answer that question myself. I'm a hunter – a tiger-hunter.'

'I'm not having my tigers shot!' shouted the head keeper. He had been sitting quietly in the audience, feeling a bit embarrassed, but now he felt he had to speak. ''We'll catch them ourselves. Just you wait and see.'

The mayor looked at him angrily.

'But we have been waiting,' he shouted out. 'And what have we seen? Nothing! All I've noticed is your men running around in circles making a lot of noise. And have they caught the tigers yet? Have they even seen them?'

The head keeper looked down at his shoes.

'Not quite,' he mumbled. 'Not yet . . .'

'Well,' said the mayor, looking towards the hunter. 'I suggest that we let somebody else have a try. What does everybody else think?'

'Yes!' they all shouted out together.

'There.' said the mayor with satisfaction. 'That settles that!'

Chapter Six

Out in the fields the next morning, the tigers romped in the long grass. They had enjoyed a good breakfast – two ducks and five hens stolen from someone's yard – and now they wanted to play. The long grass reminded them of the grass in the jungle. They could crawl through it on their stomachs, so that only the tips of their ears showed at the top, or they could jump through it in long bounds. All the things that tigers should do were coming back to them in their new-found freedom.

They moved from one field to the next. In this one the hay had been cut and was lying in large bales, waiting to be collected. Their games had tired them and so they decided to lie down beside some bales and sleep in the warmth of the morning sun.

A few hours later they woke up. There was a loud noise close by – a farmer was driving his tractor. Behind him, on a long, low trailer, were piled-up bales of hay. Mah-Var looked at Mah-Baja, who rose quietly to her feet. Quietly, unseen by the farmer, they padded behind the trailer. Then, with two quick leaps, they were up on top of the bales of hay.

It was a fine place for a tiger to be. From where they crouched on top of the hay, they had a wide view of the surrounding countryside. They could work out just where the duck runs and the hen coops were and could see the darkest places for hiding from danger.

The farmer drove on, following the hedge that ran alongside the edge of the field. After a few minutes, he stopped. Beside him on the tractor seat he had a flask of coffee, which he now poured into a tin mug and started to enjoy his mid-morning break.

Curious to find out what was happening, Mah-Baja crept forward on the top of the hay until she was directly above the farmer's head. Looking down, she saw the top of the farmer's hat directly beneath her. It was a funny old hat, battered and full of hayseeds. To a tiger it looked delicious, rather like a duck that had just been plucked.

It was just too tempting. Stretching out her paw, with its blunt old claws, Mah-Baja swiped at the top of the hat. She missed, but as her paw passed the hat, one of the claws brushed against the very top of the hat. With a normal tiger that wouldn't have mattered at all, but Mah-Baja's claws were so loose that

they were ready to come out at the slightest pull. And that was what happened. The claw lodged in the hat and popped straight out of her paw.

The farmer felt something touch his hat.

'Flies!' he muttered. 'Why on earth can't they leave me alone?'

He reached up to take off his hat to swat at the flies. And, of course, as he did so, he saw the claw sticking out of the top of the hat.

'Bless my soul!' he said in an astonished voice. 'However did that get there?'

But farmers have work to do and they don't have time to sit about asking themselves questions to which there seem to be no answer, and so the farmer started up his tractor again and off the three of them went.

When the tractor reached the end of the field, Mah-Var and Mah-Baja decided they had had enough. With one leap they were back in the long grass and heading towards the wood. Mah-Baja looked sorrowfully at her paw which had lost the claw. It was sad for a tiger to see itself falling slowly to bits, and it hurt quite a bit as well.

behind him, as he was sure to send her home if he spotted her. At the same time, she did not want to lose him.

The hunter walked slowly, looking down at the ground in front of him, stopping from time to time to examine the earth or the way in which the grass had been trampled. He knew exactly what he was looking for, and he knew how to tell the difference between the marks made by a cow walking through the grass, or a dog, and those made by a tiger.

Hiding behind a tree, Alix watched him as he dropped to his knees at the edge of a field. She saw him part the grass with his hands and peer at the ground, and she knew, with a sinking feeling in her stomach, that he had found what he was looking for.

The hunter rose to his feet and looked ahead. He had indeed seen what he wanted. There, in the dust at his feet, was a large paw-print, the unmistakable footprint of a tiger. He had seen the same sign many times before in India, and here it was again. He could tell at a glance that it had been made only a few hours before, and this meant only one thing. Not far away, perhaps only a mile or so, there was a tiger.

His rifle at the ready, the hunter began to walk slowly towards the edge of the wood. He would have to be careful, he knew, if he was to give the tiger no warning of his approach. For this reason he walked softly, making sure that he stepped on no twigs that would snap noisily. He also made sure that the wind was in the right direction. The last thing he wanted was the tigers to sniff the air and know that someone was coming. That had been the end of many tiger-hunters before him.

Alix watched in dismay as the hunter moved slowly towards the wood. If she was going to do anything, she knew that she would have to do it quickly. But what? The idea came to her suddenly.

'Tigers!' she shouted at the top of her voice. 'I've seen the tigers!'

The hunter spun round to see Alix running from behind the tree, waving her arms vigorously. Quickly he slung his rifle over his shoulder and ran to join her.

'Where?' he said breathlessly. 'Where did you see the tigers?'

Alix pointed away from the wood.

'I saw them going towards that farm,' she replied. 'They shot through the grass. I nearly missed them.'

The hunter looked doubtful. 'Are you sure they went that way?' he asked. 'Are you certain that they didn't go towards the wood?'

'I'm sure of it,' Alix said. 'Absolutely sure.'

'Well,' said the hunter. 'Go home immediately and stay indoors. Girls shouldn't be wandering around when there are tigers about.'

Alix nodded and obediently set off in the direction of home. The hunter, his rat-like face set in a look of determination, started off again, heading away from the wood in the direction in which Alix had seen no tigers going.

Chapter Eight

Nobody saw the tigers the next day, nor the day after that. But on the following day, which was a Wednesday, the most terrible thing happened.

Alix was at school, sitting quietly through a mathematics lessons, wondering when it was going to end. She tried to follow what was happening on the board, but her gaze kept wandering. Her seat was near a window, and the things which happened outside always seemed to be more interesting than mathematics.

Suddenly she caught her breath. She had seen something move outside in the schoolyard. She could not be exactly sure what it was, but it was certainly something big. There had been a flash of yellow, a dash of black, a moving shadow. Alix craned her neck to see more, but there seemed to be nothing.

Then, when she had shifted her gaze back into the classroom, from the very corner of her eye she saw another movement. This time it was

unmistakable. She had seen a tiger.

Alix wondered what to do. Should she tell the teacher that there was a tiger in the schoolyard? Should she keep quiet? Should she slip out and try to frighten it away? She glanced across the room to where her friend John sat. Would he carry out his threat to tell everybody that she had let the tigers out?

Even if Alix had made up her mind, she would not have had time to do anything. With an awful bang, the classroom door was pushed open and there, framed in the doorway, his great mouth open, stood Mah-Var.

For a moment there was absolute silence. Then people began to scream. Mah-Var stood, immobile. He could hardly hear the screams, so deaf was he, and so there was no reason for him to be frightened. All he saw was a group of people jumping around, waving their hands. It was really no different from the zoo, only this time he was on the outside looking in.

After a few moments the teacher's voice could be heard above the general din.

'Keep calm,' she shouted. And then, as the noise subsided, she went on: 'Very, very slowly, everybody is to climb up on to the shelves and the tops of the cupboards.'

Nobody needed to be told twice, and soon the entire class, including the teacher, was perched up on top of the shelves and cupboards that lined the classroom. It made a very strange sight, but it did mean that if the tiger wanted to bite anybody it would have to jump to do it.

Mah-Var watched, unmoving. Then, with the faintest of roars, which

nonetheless sounded quite loud in the confines of the classroom, he strolled into the room, closely followed by Mah-Baja.

'Don't scream!' screamed the teacher. 'Don't move!'

Alix watched in horror as the two tigers made their way to the middle of the room, sniffing at the desk-legs, swishing their tails against the chairs. On the other side of the room she could see John on top of the map cupboard. He caught her glance and frowned angrily back at her. She could tell exactly what he was thinking. Your fault!

Mah-Var went to the front of the room and put his paws up on the teacher's table. As he did so, he sent all her books and papers flying. Mah-Baja gave a growl when this happened, but she was too busy ripping open a schoolbag to pay too much attention.

Had the tigers not found the school lunches, then it is likely that they would have wandered out again. But when Mah-Baja found the sandwich pack which somebody had knocked off a table, they both set about them with glee. Alix watched as they ripped off the paper with their teeth and munched their way through the contents, sending fragments of bread and paper flying in all directions.

After a few minutes the two tigers had had their fill and began to pace about the room again.

'They're going to eat one of us,' one of the children said. 'The sandwiches were just the first course.'

At this John shouted out, 'I hope they eat Alix first. She deserves it!'

'That's not very nice,' called out the teacher. 'Just because there are tigers in the room, that doesn't mean that . . .'

She did not finish what she was going to say, as the tigers, disturbed by the voices, bounded towards the door. As suddenly as they had arrived, they were gone, leaving a roomful of shaken people slowly beginning to climb down from their perches.

'You've got two days,' John hissed to Alix. 'If you don't catch those tigers within two days, I'm going to do what I said I'd do.' He laughed. 'See you in prison!'

Chapter Nine

After the incident in the classroom, the tiger-hunter was asked by the mayor to redouble his efforts.

'We can't let that happen again,' the mayor warned. 'You really must shoot those animals.'

The hunter nodded. 'Don't worry,'

he said. 'I'm picking up their tracks all over the place. It's only a matter of time before I catch up with them.'

Alix was more worried than ever before. She lay awake at night wondering how on earth she could capture the tigers when the experienced tiger-hunter was having no success. She toyed with the idea of running away. If she did that, then it wouldn't matter if John carried out his threat to tell everyone that she was responsible for the tigers being on the loose in the first place. But it was easier to think about running away than to put such a plan into operation. Where would she run to? She had no idea of where people went when they ran away. In books, they went to sea, or to foreign lands. But could one do that these days? She thought not.

Then, quite suddenly, an idea came to her. She remembered the way the tigers had behaved in the classroom. They had seemed to be most interested in one thing: food. When the children had all come down from their safe places on the cupboards and shelves, Alix and two others had been given the task of clearing up the mess that the tigers had made of the lunches. She had noticed something odd about the jumble of broken sandwiches that lay scattered about the floor. Some of the sandwiches had been left untouched. All the peanut-butter ones had not even been licked. One or two jam sandwiches had clearly been tasted but had then been spat out, covered with tiger tooth-marks. Some sandwiches, though, had been gobbled right up. These were the chicken ones.

So the tigers obviously loved chicken. And if they liked chicken so much, then that might be the way to lure them into some sort of trap. Alix sat up in bed and turned on her light. A trap? A trap?

She whooped with delight as the whole plan unravelled before her. Yes! Yes! That would be the way to catch the tigers. Relieved at the thought that her problems were over, Alix turned off her light again and was soon asleep. In her dreams, Mah-Var and Mah-Baja romped and rolled in

open fields, happy at last, calling out to her to join them.

The most difficult part of the plan was the buying of the chicken. Alix had thought at first that she would buy a number of chickens that had already been roasted, but when she saw what this would cost she had to give up that idea. For a few minutes she thought that her plan would have to be abandoned at this stage, but then she saw the small chicken pies all neatly laid out on the counter of the shop with a large sign saying 'Special Offer'.

The shopkeeper was rather surprised to see Alix buy quite so many pies, but he thought that she was probably planning a picnic for her friends and so he wrapped them all in silver foil and put them in a large bag. Alix thanked him and left the shop. That was the first stage of the plan. Now for the second.

Like most plans, of course, Alix's plan became more difficult as it went along. The next thing that she had to do was to wait until dark. She could not go out until then as too many people would see her and begin to wonder what she was doing. It was essential for the success of the plan that everything was kept very, very secret.

At last the afternoon began to fade into evening and Alix was able to leave her house and set out for the woods where she knew the tigers were likely to be lurking. In her large red sports bag she carried the carefully cut up chicken pies and in her pocket she had tucked one of her father's torches. Although it was dark, she did not use the torch, making her way instead by the faint light that came from the night sky.

As she reached the edge of the woods, she glanced over her shoulder to see if there was anybody about. The last thing she wanted, of course, was for somebody to come up to her and say, 'What have you got in that bag?' or, 'Why are you going up to the woods?'

Darkness came very quickly and the woods were soon a great black mass in front of her. She shivered a little and wondered whether she should go ahead with the plan. It would be so easy to turn back now. It would be so easy to run back through the brightly lit streets and forget all about this. But could she really do that? She owed it to the tigers to capture them, to save them from the hunter. If she didn't find them tonight, then in a few days' time they were bound to end up as rugs.

Alix stopped when she reached the edge of the wood. Drawing in a deep breath, she looked at the path ahead of her. She could use the torch safely now, but even that was such a tiny beam of light in the echoing blackness.

She felt her way slowly along the

path. All about her there were shadows and dark shapes, any one of which might have been a lurking tiger. There were noises too, strange noises, swishing sounds, bumps, the sort of sounds that tigers might well make as they crept through the darkness.

She tried not to think about it, but the thought of being eaten would not leave her mind. I hope it's quick, she said to herself. I hope that they don't take their time swallowing me.

At last she reached the very middle of the woods. It was a terrible place, a small clearing completely surrounded by a wall of trees. If anything dreadful were to happen, then this surely was the most likely place for it to take place.

Fumbling in her bag, she took out a handful of chicken pie pieces and began to retrace her steps down the path. Every so often she put a piece of pie down on the pathway, making a long trail that led from the centre of the woods to the outside. When she reached the place where the path emerged from the trees, she breathed a sigh of relief.

'I've done it,' she said, her voice sounding very loud in the darkness.

Now the rest was simple. Still laying a trail of chicken pieces, she struck out from the edge of the wood to the farmyard across the field. She could see the lights of the farmhouse in the distance, but there did not seem to be any other sign of life. Opening the farm gate, she made her way to the large barn not far away, taking the chicken pie trail right up to the front door and into the barn itself. There on the floor towards the back of the barn, she tipped out the remaining pieces of chicken in one delicious heap. It would be a great reward for any tiger who had patiently followed the trail.

Chapter Ten

Deep in the heart of the woods, the tigers prowled through the undergrowth. They were not in a good mood. The farmers had become worried about the loss of their chickens and ducks and had locked them all away in barns. It was two days since they had had a good meal and their stomachs were rumbling with hunger. Of course there were rabbits in the woods, lovely juicy rabbits, but they were too quick for the tigers who would never be able to catch them.

Suddenly Mah-Baja stopped. Raising her nose in the air, she took a deep breath. Yes. There was something there – a familiar smell, an enticing smell. Mah-Var came up behind her and looked at the other tiger inquisitively. He too raised his nose in the air, his whiskers twitching as he took the scent.

Slowly Mah-Baja moved off in the direction of the clearing. As she approached it, the scent became stronger and she broke into a gentle run. She had now recognized the scent and her mouth was watering. It was chicken – it could be nothing other than chicken!

It did not take the two tigers long to gobble up the pieces of chicken pie that lay about the clearing. Then, their noses telling them infallibly that there was more to be had, they set off down the path. Piece of chicken pie by piece of chicken pie, they made their way along the trail which Alix had set. They gave no thought to what the delicious morsels were doing lying on the path; all they knew was that their silent prayers for chicken had been royally answered. Perhaps the trail would go on forever – a tiger's dream.

Out in the open field, the tigers

became more cautious. Now they looked about them before they lowered their heads to guzzle up the chicken, but there seemed to be no danger. Gradually they drew nearer to the farmyard and, after the slightest hesitation, slunk through the gate.

From a hiding place behind some rain-barrels, Alix watched the tigers creep into the farmyard. In the dark, they seemed larger than she had remembered them and she hoped that they would not see her. The tigers, however, were intent on one thing only – finding more chicken.

Mah-Baja picked up the last of the pieces in the yard and looked about her. She and Mah-Var were now

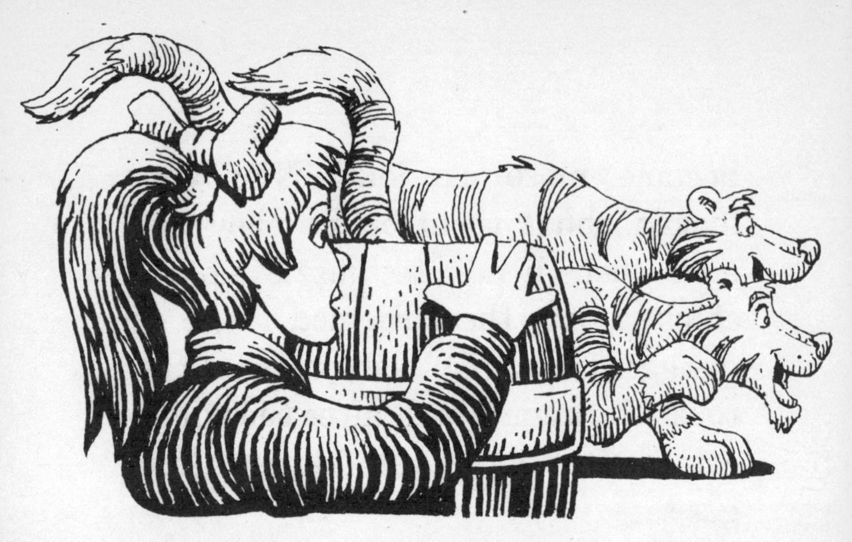

standing directly in front of the barn door and their noses told them that if they wanted more they would have to go inside. Mah-Var peered into the darkness of the barn. Would it be safe? Could there be danger lurking inside? What was that big dark shape in the corner?

'Go on,' Alix muttered under her breath. 'Please go inside!'

Mah-Baja gave a bit of a growl, just

to warn anything that might be inside that it should get out of the way. And then, closely followed by Mah-Var, she crept into the barn.

As the last of Mah-Var's tail disappeared round the edge of the door, Alix ran out from her hiding place. Her heart thumping within her, she seized the barn door and, using all her strength, slammed it shut. Then, with a quick movement of her wrist, she slipped the catch into place.

'That's it,' she said. 'I've caught them.'

No sooner had the catch fallen into position than there came a mighty roar from within the barn. Then, within a second or two, there was a great thump against the door. Alix felt the wood bump into her as the weight of the tigers battered against the struts of the door. Bang! A pause, and then bump! Crunch!

Alix leant against the door, trying to keep it from bursting open. She noticed that the catch was coming undone under the tigers' onslaught and she tried desperately to keep it in. She knew, though, that she would not be able to imprison them for long. And then . . .

'Help!' she shouted out. 'Tigers!'

Her voice seemed so tiny against the noise that the tigers were creating inside that she thought it most unlikely that anybody would hear her. But it was all that she could do. If she left the door and ran away, the tigers would soon burst it open and come after her. And yet, if she stayed, they would soon break it down anyway. Either way, everything seemed hopeless.

If the farmer had not come out to feed his dog, then he probably would not have heard Alix's cry for help. When he did hear it, though, he lost no time in rushing across to the barn.

'Whatever's going on?' he asked breathlessly.

Alix told him quickly that there were tigers in his barn. When he heard this, without wasting any time he fetched several heavy barrels from across the farmyard and wedged them in front of the barn door.

'That should help,' he said. 'Now

you go quickly up to the farmhouse and telephone the zoo. Tell them we've got their tigers but that we won't have them for long!'

Chapter Eleven

It did not take the zoo-keepers long to reach the farm. They drove so quickly that on the way their truck knocked down two road signs and one postbox. But there they were, with a large steel cage which they unloaded from the truck and placed directly outside the barn door.

'Now,' said the head keeper. 'This will be easy. All we do is open the barn door and let the tigers run out into the cage. Then I slam that shut and there we are – two tigers, safely caged, incapable of causing any more trouble.'

The farmer looked doubtful and Alix felt more than a little worried. Was the cage big enough? she wondered. What if they slipped round the side?

At last everything was ready and the head keeper signalled to the farmer to take the catch off the barn door. For a moment or two nothing happened, but then, with a sudden rush, the door burst open and the tigers bounded out. The head keeper gave shout of triumph and pulled a small lever which shut the door of the cage.

'There!' he yelled. 'It's worked!'

Realizing that he was in a cage, Mah-Var started to give a roar of anger. Somehow, however, it came out as more of a squeak. He just did not have the energy to escape all over again. He was too old.

Mah-Baja looked about her and sat down. There was no point in making a fuss. This was the end of her freedom, and she knew it.

The news of the capture of the tigers soon got round the town. There was a public meeting to announce the fact officially, and the mayor made a speech in which much was made of Alix's bravery.

'If everybody were like her,' the mayor said, 'then this town would be a different place.'

Everybody clapped loudly, except for Alix, who was embarrassed by all the fuss and wished that the whole thing would be forgotten as soon as possible.

'You don't have to thank me,' she told the mayor later. 'I had to do it. After all, it was my fault they were out to begin with.'

The mayor looked at her and raised an eyebrow. Then he burst out laughing. 'Your fault? Ha, ha. That's a good joke. Oh yes. Your fault. Ha, ha.'

Alix shrugged her shoulders. She'd told the truth; if the mayor chose to think it was a joke, then there was not much she could do about that.

At school the principal made a speech as well.

'You're a credit to us all,' he said, beaming at Alix. Once again, everybody clapped, even John. He had been so impressed by the story of Alix's bravery that he had come to apologize.

As for the tigers, they went back to the zoo, but not for long. The mayor was so cross about the whole affair that he told the head keeper that it would be better if the zoo didn't keep tigers any more. So the tigers were sent to another, much better zoo,

some distance away. There they had a splendid, much larger cage, with several good trees on which to sharpen their remaining teeth and claws. It was not quite as good as being free, of course, but they were well fed and happy and so it was probably the next best thing.

Alix visited them there one day. She peered through the bars of their comfortable new pen and tried to attract Mah-Baja's attention. But the sun was warm and Mah-Baja was far too sleepy to bother about visitors. Alix didn't mind.